THE EXPLODING TREE

STORIES

KEVIN RICHARD WHITE

Copyright © 2024 Kevin Richard White

All rights reserved. No part of this publication may be reproduced, distributed, or transmitted in any form or by any means, including photocopying, recording, or other electronic or mechanical methods, without the prior written permission of the publisher, except in the case of brief quotations embodied in critical reviews and certain other non-commercial uses permitted by copyright law.

Front cover image/ interior design by:

ANXIETY DRIVEN GRAPHICS

ISBN: 9798878718707

CONTENTS

15 CHRISTMAS COMMERCIALS

19 THE EXPLODING TREE

24 COME AND SEE THIS

25 SMOKE AND TEA

35 DEAD MACHINE

39 BARN FIRE, 1985

43 HAM AND CHEESE ON WHEAT

47 STOP TELLING ME I'M BEAUTIFUL

62 FISH GHOST

69 THICKER SKIN

75 THE BOAT OVER THERE

81 BAD DAY

100 WE CAN REGAIN ABILITY IN TERRIFIC WAYS

104 THE RACES

110 IT'S ALL ABOUT THE BREATHING

119 THE OLD BRIDE

127 THERE'S NO ONE HERE BY THAT NAME

129 THE BEST AMERICAN DEATHS OF THE LAST YEAR

AUTHOR'S NOTE

Slightly edited versions of these pieces were previously published in the following publications. This author is very grateful to said publications:

christmas commercials - *The Hunger*

the exploding tree - *X-R-A-Y*

come and see this - *Rejection Letters*

smoke and tea - *Grub Street*

dead machine - *Rejection Letters*

barn fire, 1985 - *Barren Magazine*

ham and cheese on wheat - *SVJ Lit*

stop telling me i'm beautiful - *The Hunger*

fish ghost - *X-R-A-Y*

thicker skin - *decomP*

the boat over there - *Death of Print*

bad day - *The Broadkill Review*

we can regain ability in terrific ways - *Rejection Letters*

the races - *Back Patio Press*

it's all about the breathing - *Hypertext*

the old bride - *The Helix*

there's no one here by that name - *Rejection Letters*

the best american deaths of the last year - *Tahoe Valley Writers Works*

ACKNOWLEDGMENTS

For Jenn - thank you for never giving up on me. I love you.

For Tim - best brother I could ever ask for.

For Seth - for always reading.

"If you have to, let yourself imagine the mood of this story, the places it might happen, what the weather will be like. Tell yourself it will be a world, at least, where you're less abandoned, and sustained by more than illusion. If you have to. Just leave before you change your mind."

-NIC PIZZOLATTO, "BETWEEN HERE AND THE YELLOW SEA"

THE EXPLODING TREE

CHRISTMAS COMMERCIALS

He was selling his dead wife's jewelry. He cut a pathetic figure, a schlub on a bender.

"I got no need for it," he said.

"I'd rather have another vodka," I said. "I'm not a frills person."

"It's from Jeweler's Row."

He pulled a silver band out of an Acme bag.

"Find a pawn shop."

"Can't get a beer at a pawn shop," he said. "Figured I'd come here."

I decided to bite. The game wasn't on yet anyway. "Okay. How did she die?"

"I begged her to wake up," he said instead.

"I'm guessing she didn't."

"She didn't," he said. "Ah, fuck it."

There was more vodka. Time broke and spilled onto this surface we sat at.

"Alright. I'll buy the silver band," I said after an hour.

He looked fit to weep. "Excellent," he said.

Later, we sat in the dark on my couch, unsure and dehydrated. I fiddled with the silver band. I waited for him to compliment me. After all, I did bring him home. I wanted to choke him, just to hear a sound, but he stayed silent, focusing on the television instead of my arm.

"Does this look as good on me as it did on her?" I said.

He shrugged. "I'm not really sure. Her skin was more tan than yours."

I could have annihilated him.

An awful Macy's commercial came on, with perfect white people happily throwing presents and fake snow around. He started to laugh.

"What?"

He pointed, a thin spittle of saliva hanging from his lip from the laugh. "These Christmas commercials. Aren't they fucking bullshit?"

I wondered if she hated him, how long she debated annihilating him, if her tan skin smothered him on beds.

"Aren't they?" He turned to me.

I nodded, then pushed him back on the couch. I unzipped his pants and put my hand down in and made sure to say nothing. I began to move.

"She did it faster," he said after a moment.

He turned to look at me, but I held his neck with my other forearm.

"I can't look at your eyes anymore," I said. "Just watch the screen."

I emulated speed. I moved. I looked down at my wrist. The jewelry looked nice. His wife had good taste. I wished she was resting peacefully.

He made a childish moan. It wasn't a sound a real man would have made.

On the TV, a voice said, "Only now at Macy's."

THE EXPLODING TREE

She's feeding you the remains of her meal. Like you're some animal child.

There's a tattoo of an exploding tree on her back and right shoulder blade: black ink paint splatter on her smooth skin, roots pulled up, snapped branches, drifting leaves that become new birds. Hair covers it, but not often.

One day you woke up and it was there. You were angry about it at first, but then you realized you had a lot in common with that tree: you both couldn't move and had nowhere to go fast.

You open your mouth. You want more of the dry chicken she has cooked, but she has thrown it away. You beg to suck on at least a bone, but she whispers, "No". She takes you out of your chair and lays you down on your belly. You're a fish again, one of your favorite playtime activities.

After she got the tattoo, you watched from the bed as she cleaned it, kept it moisturized, watched the pitch blackness brighten her skin. You wish you had hands to help her, or at least trace it, make a shape of it to keep. But you watch. And shake. How can something so artistic be out of your grasp. She continues to smooth her skin and you want to scream.

You're a man of broken parts. She's your mechanic. Somewhere, along the line, the manual will be written to make you a new human being again. It could take days or years, but she has promised you, in mellow voices, that you'll have hands again. That you'll have it all back. But you think and never tell her that you're past the warranty date.

On your belly, you imagine you're a guppy, cascading through dark warm water. She rubs your back and shoulders, trying to get knots out. Perhaps she is trying to give you a tree tattoo of your own, you think. You try to say this but fish don't talk and so you just continue to think you're swimming until she's done.

She could have left a long time ago, you told her once. There's no need to take care of me like this. But she smiled. And in response, she whispers, "Well then, who would take care of me?"

After you're done being a fish, she goes to get you ready for bed. Pajamas on, teeth brushed, and sets up the laptop for you to use. She puts the mouth operated mouse in and you're good to watch movies for as long as you want. She goes to get ready herself for her job. You watch her undress. The tree is there, shining. She puts on her black dress and bracelets and brushes her hair. She leaves the tree visible this time, usually covering it up. That's when you can't take it anymore. You spit out the mouse.

"Don't let anyone touch that tonight," you say.

She spins around, still brushing. "Touch what?"

"Your tattoo."

She smiles. "You're a silly boy."

"I'm serious. It's yours. Don't let anyone touch it."

"It's yours, too, baby."

She comes over and kisses you. The smell leaves you breathless. Your mechanic. The one who feeds you. The one with perfect hands that are replacing yours.

She puts the mouse back in so you can operate the computer again. Before she leaves for the night, she kisses you one more time, and wants you to sleep well. She'll be back later, she says. The door shuts. You're still hungry, but have to wait.

After some time, you fall asleep, thinking you're still a guppy. Back through rivers and past sharks, you're going towards some kind of light. When you get there, it's a small island, white sand, shells and crabs. But there's one tree. A large black one that reaches to the ceiling of the sky. Suddenly, you're an animal, climbing up. You get to the top. Leaves drift and become birds. You want to soar like them. The tree gets blacker against the blue sky, and you reach a claw out, breathing hard, wishing it becomes a wing. They all continue to softly drift up and over the water, and as you pray to fly, you hear an explosion from under you, bomb-like. Something lifts. You fly, but not well.

COME AND SEE THIS

He had to use the bathroom. Mom and Dad were right there in the backyard, so I let him in.

I was playing with my Legos. I wanted to show him my pirate ship. I knocked.

"Come and see this," I said. I tried opening the door but it was like something fell against it.

Mom and Dad came back. I told them the postman was in the bathroom. Dad started taking the doorknob off. Mom called 911. I went back to the tub for the pirate figures. But I couldn't find them and I was getting frustrated.

SMOKE AND TEA

She took the last swallow of her wine. She set the glass on the floor and it fell over right away.

"What," she asked him.

"I didn't say anything," he said back.

She shut her eyes and ran a hand over her face and through her hair. She was no longer pretty.

She wanted to cut her wings and be unable to fly. She imagined it a bloody affair, but she did not want to clean it up afterward.

"That was good," she finally said, not really meaning it.

"I'm going to get some water," he said, standing up.

"I don't want any."

"Whatever you say," he said left the room behind.

Seconds masqueraded as minutes. Her brain went someplace vile. Frenzied. She fingered and toyed with an old piece of skin on her palm.

He came back with tea.

"That's not water."

"No," he said, sitting back down. His shirt was a size too small. Cheap fabric. On sale. Did his mother buy it, she wondered?

She laughed.

"Want to share?"

"Share what?"

"The joke."

The dead skin fell to the floor. She will make a new layer soon.

"I'd like a smoke," she said finally.

"I didn't say smoke."

"Oh."

"I said joke."

"Hmmm," was all she said.

Once when she was a volunteer, someone put a hand on her shoulder and asked her if she felt that love and peace began in the bedroom, or if not that, where would she prefer it began? He was the first of many, to ruin her causes, to infect what she held dear. She fell for them - boring men who wanted their time, and then they're gone, like light crawling away. Now she does not volunteer. All she did was wonder where he bought his shirts.

"Is that unsweetened?"

"Yes, it is," he answered.

"I think I do want a glass after all."

"In a minute," he said, taking off his glasses to rub his eyes.

She thought about how she would cut her wings. Temporarily she considered those scissors you use in elementary art class. One zig-zag like, one squiggly, one jagged. But she didn't know which one should give the best cut. So she abandoned the idea. She thought maybe it would be better if she would burn them off.

"What did that man say to you," he started, "when you left the riot?"

"It wasn't a riot. It was a protest."

"So you say."

"We were protesting."

He sipped his tea, thought about her dressing in white for a change.

"We were fighting for equality."

"Hmm," he said.

"Can I have more wine?"

"No."

She sighed, wanting a new scar to call hers.

"We were anarchists."

"That's a casual term."

"No, it isn't," she spat back.

The tea was not good, but he did not want to get up again. Even to see her from another angle. But what does that prove even if he did?

"I don't want to talk about those days."

"What days?"

"Don't make me say it."

"Well, then," he said, "what do you want to talk about?"

She paused.

Age, going in and out like waves, like wind bleeding through the holes in drywall and stucco. Sounds laughing their way into walls of bedrooms, where her hands, collecting rings and stress lines, grasp-clutch the wrinkled, drunken skin of causeless, vapid strangers. Complex pieces of time, they are. They don't want to be cured, they are meant to stay in your head, a fog like a friend, blurry and pointed, along for the ride.

She did not want to go back to her evening GED class.

"My wings," she said.

He took a swallow of semi-warm tea.

"What wings?" He asked softly.

"When I was younger," she started, "I used to be able to fly."

"How did you know this?"

"You're told, when you're younger. Or at least you see it. On those fucking posters on the walls in kindergarten. With the squiggly scissors. And I used to have wings, but I let them get ratty. I didn't care. So I let them die. And I want to get rid of them."

"Why don't you try, then," he said, picking a piece of lint off his shirt, "to take better care of them and fly again?"

"I don't know the path. I forget where shit is. Or rather, where it goes. I'd really like another glass of wine."

"Will you tell me then about the riot?"

"I guess. Sure."

He got up and walked to the cabinet, limping as he did. He knew she would ask if he was alright, so he said, "It's an old baseball injury."

"What is? The wine?"

He chuckled. She didn't get it. "Never mind."

"Where did you get your degree?"

He poured her a healthy glass. "I want to get back to these wings. I want to know why you stopped taking care of them. They seem like a good thing to have."

"They're a fucking pain in the ass," she said as she took the glass from him and drank from it liberally.

"Careful," he warned her. "You have class tonight."

"I was too busy listening to others," she said. "And I forgot that I make opinions, too. I wanted to make my own but I fell in love with the opinions of others. And the sex was amazing. Everything made sense, briefly. And I'm lost now, because I forgot what it's like to move on my own, to go places where others haven't been. Do you know what I mean?"

"Sure, I do," he nodded. He let the tea go. He yawned and tapped his pen on his notepad. He wanted to write something meaningful but when language is broken, what else can you use to convey love?

"I don't think you do," she said, downing the wine, dropping the glass, and stopping to tie her shoe. "I don't think you know what it's like to feel love. Or to know what good sex is. What it's like to fight for causes. It's easy for you to sit here and judge me because you're high above me. But you're not. I could be a million times smarter than you. What makes you so special?"

Once he smelled her perfume. Once she wore a skirt with boots. Both times he wanted to take matters in his own hands and make love to her like she talked about. But he did not because he was honest. He suddenly cared deeply for her because she had wings she did not tend to, and he wanted to give her a care package so she could fly.

He straightened his tie and looked at her. "When I was younger, I once put a BB gun to my heart. My dad's BB gun. It was loaded. I shook it. It looked like an old Revolutionary war pistol. A flintlock. And the fucker was heavy. Anyway, I decided to try it. I don't know how old I was. I wasn't even suicidal. What did I know of damage then? Nothing. Anyway, I put it to my heart. The safety was on. That's when I knew that was love. Was my father a smart man for keeping loaded weapons around, where his kids could get them with ease? No. But did he know something about love? Sure. And trust? Most definitely. Maybe that's what you need. Instead of this projection of love. Maybe you need someone to put a gun to your heart. So you can feel what it's like to feel the fear of love. That's what I call that moment. A fear of love. Both things at once. It was a moment that I could never recreate. I tried once, with my own gun. But it wasn't the same. I put the gun back and it doesn't come back out because it scares my wife. But why be scared of love? Doesn't it fix things? Doesn't it make things...sound better?"

She watched him for a while. She did not know what to do. The wine swam in her stomach and made cannonballs. She would not make it to her evening class. She wanted a million and one things, but the armchair in the office seemed to be the most stable platform in the city.

"What kind of therapist are you?" She asked him quietly, with a trace of admiration faintly audible in her voice.

He laughed.

DEAD MACHINE

Our bartender just died, the gap-toothed woman told me. Do you think you can hop in for a few days.

Well, I said. How did he die?

What does it matter? Beer glasses are over there.

I had just gotten into town. I needed a new carburetor. I guessed this was how I was going to get it.

I asked the old guy at the end how the old bartender died.

I don't know, he said. I think he smoked.

You're smoking, I said.

Bored. Dying sounds good, he said.

So for two days I worked. I poured flat beer horribly. It all went down like Communion. I got wrinkled dollar bills. I shoved them in my shirt pocket.

I found out the mechanic couldn't get a carburetor in for a week.

So Amazon Prime it, I said.

Amazon Prime don't come out here, the mechanic said. Tobacco juice dribbled onto the buttons on his denim shirt.

Fucking do something then, I said. I'm not a bartender.

But I poured. I listened. God, did I ever listen. War stories from pacifists. I dreamed of my past world. I had been a taxi driver in Chicago. Drove around show ladies with cum in their mouth, day traders with pizza grease on their clip-ons. I'm not saying I enjoyed it. But it made sense.

I started to get cheated on pay. I went to the gap-toothed lady.

I'm being stiffed, I said.

Then quit watching so much porn, she said. And laughed. It smelled like garbage.

I slept with a crooked neck in the backseat of my dead machine. I wanted to amble on, sway with the grass and not think about the show ladies. That night, I dreamt I was a smoky pile of cum in the gap-toothed lady's mouth. When I tried to escape, I choked her, which I admit brought me a laugh.

After the week was up, I found the mechanic.

Got my carburetor?

Ah shit, man, he said, smacking his head like a cartoon character. I forgot to order it.

You forgot to fucking what, I said.

I knew I was forgetting something:

I have every right to kill you, I said. You son of a bitch.

Look, man, I'll do it now. I'll get on the phone. I will. I'll get on the phone.

Motherfucker, I said, as he ambled away.

Maybe the old guy in the bar was right. Maybe dying was the thing to do. It made me think of the bartender, the one no one would tell me about. Maybe he died like a friend of mine did. I won't say where we were or what we were doing. But it was kind of gross. Sad and spectacular. It reminded me of how water dries up on hot macadam.

BARN FIRE, 1985

Back in October 1985, I woke up to the horses dying.

My parents weren't home - they were spending the last of their paychecks line dancing and whiskey-tasting. They could be blamed for a lot, but there was no way this could be pinned on them. I never did find out how it started, but that's not what's important about this.

My sister Laurie woke me up. She was cleaning up from the spaghetti dinner we had earlier that night. "Ben, wake up," she cooed into my ear. She was calm, but I could smell the whiskey on her breath too - she was fond of sneaking sips when she was in charge. "Get dressed."

I heard the howls from the animals glide along in a windstream through our backyard and into my open window. It was an odd song, one you might hear when you're locked into a nightmare. I couldn't find my shirt. Laurie grabbed my hand anyway and we opened the screen door.

Our property was not big so right away we were hit with wood ash and ember and the sounds of the livestock. I never saw a fire brighter. I heard it sing and whistle as I saw the smoke rise up and disappear into the nighttime with the few stars that were out. The animals, though, were louder. I remember them being throaty and harrowed, unjust and roaring.

"There's nothing we can do," Laurie said as I started to walk towards it. I'll never forget the pitch her voice had, the glaze in her eyes. She was right. Calling the firemen would have been impossible - our parents had forgotten to pay the phone bill and our neighbors didn't like us enough to look out for us. Reputation can be a terrible thing.

I watched as cracked wood fell. She stifled a sob as she thought of all that was in there - her favorite pony, the hay bales we jumped into from the loft. I tried to run towards it again, but she tackled me into the ground and I spent the rest of the night picking wet grass off my chest and neck. The fire showed no signs of slowing down its performance. It shone like rare gold, throwing out its expanse over everything that lay around.

I was trying to count the number of bones we would have to throw in garbage bags when it was all said and done. I only hoped some had made it out, whether through a slit or by luck, but I wasn't holding my breath.

I don't know how long we stood there but I heard the crunch and whirring of Dad's pickup truck. I turned and there they were, hanging onto each other like vines, drunk as hell and also struck by the sight of their livelihood tumbling down. Laurie tried to hug them but they acted like stone, not interested in love or affection. Mom went into the house after a pause and I figured I'd try to talk it out, make sense of it all.

"Dad, all the horses were in there."

This is what is important about this story.

He didn't look at me. I saw fire in his eyes. Eventually, he ruffled my hair but that was it.

Mom came back outside with the whiskey bottle that Laurie had been sipping from and gathered us all into a huddle.

"Well," she said as she unscrewed the cap, "what are we going to drink to?"

Laurie laughed, unsure, like she couldn't believe it.

Dad gave a hearty bellow and took the bottle, drank a big swig. He acted like he was going to say something, but kept his mouth shut again. He offered the bottle to the both of us. Laurie shook her head and walked away, picking bits of wood and whatever else off of her clothes. I took the bottle in my hand, couldn't believe what I was doing.

"You're a man now, I guess," Dad said.

I took a drink - my first and last one. I couldn't help it. It was too much like the fire that I just saw.

When I finally went back in, Mom and Dad were slow-dancing, like they were in a ballroom. There was still screaming.

HAM AND CHEESE ON WHEAT

Dad was at it again.

"I miss that dog. He was friendlier than Mom, I'll tell you that."

"That was eighteen years ago, Dad."

He was in the kitchen, fumbling around. A wisp in a tight flannel shirt. Not drunk, just acting fucking weird. Opening and closing cabinet doors, scratching a non-existent beard. He started fighting with the bread box. I walked into the kitchen, took my beer with me. I reached behind him and opened the bread box door. He was on finicky legs. I pushed him aside gently and grabbed the wheat bread, undid the tie.

"You want ham and cheese?"

"Will, everything that has lived in my life. It's been alive. But now it's…"

"Come on, man." I didn't know what else to say.

"I'm sorry, I…"

"Don't apologize, Dad."

"I know, but…it's so weird. My memory…It goes like a wave. Sloshes around. And then it's gone. I don't know how else to word it."

I waited for him to at least try while I made his sandwich. But he didn't talk. I looked out the kitchen window ahead of me as I did. Snow. Getting darker out and we had nowhere to go. I moved back when Mom moved on. Doing my part as the loving, doting son. Because no one else would. No one else could.

"Look, I'm sure as God made little green apples that…I got a bad hand here. In life. Mom and that dog."

"Well, then if Mom's a bad hand, then I'm the bad fucking card, because here I am, making your sandwich."

"Will, that's not what I meant…I…" And I turned and there he was, scratching a non-existent beard. I almost yelled at him to rip that tight flannel shirt off. I gave him the unfinished sandwich with no plate. I sat there with my beer and watched him drop crumbs all over himself. I had a haze going.

"The dog," he said between bites.

"Christ, who gives a fuck? Got hit by a truck. What other chapter do you want to add to that story?"

I sat there and finished my beer while I waited. My dad was always a terrible shot. In the Gulf War, he missed every target. Said he never adapted to the weight of a rifle. But fuck, does he know the weight of a bullet. Because he went for the kill and it was gorgeous.

"Well, then...what about Lauren?"

"What about her?"

My voice got hard, like a fall down the steps.

He chewed. He sat stoic. "Shouldn't you get over it, too? Isn't that why you're here?"

"No, Dad," I said quietly.

"To get over your wife. Who I liked more than the dog, actually."

"Dad, shut the fuck up."

Dad knew he fired right. He sat in the chair, slowly eating the sandwich. I thought more about Lauren and her soft skin. My eyes expanded. Dad was not thinking about soft skin. He was thinking of dog hair and death. He stuck his hand out and I saw the sandwich half taunting me.

"Want half?"

STOP TELLING ME I'M BEAUTIFUL

It was strange watching my husband start a fire. It looked like his limbs were newly attached just this morning.

"Well, what do you want me to tell you?" he said, crumbling up newspaper from the kindling box.

"Tell me anything. Tell me that your heart is a mess. Or that you hate sunsets. You can tell me anything you want and it would be better than anything you said to me this entire year. Just be honest with me."

"I'm always honest with you, Ellie."

I snorted. We were the only ones in the lounge, which is why this conversation was taking place. I looked out the window and took note of the Applachians. All I saw was white on the ground and dark in the air. It weighed on top of me like a down blanket and I didn't want to get rid of it. I looked back at him and he was watching me, carefully, like I was an old bat who was losing his mind. Maybe I was. I always feared that I would. I spent a lifetime doing dumb things. Like coming here. Like being in a love I couldn't hold right.

"I thought you would have had this fire roaring by now," I told him. "Enough to cook a whole damn bag of marshmallows."

He sighed and balled up some more, threw it like a baseball at the kindling already in there.

"Well, go on," I said. "You only told everyone else in the whole place already."

"I didn't say it was my hidden talent or anything. Yeesh. Let it go, babe."

I let it drop. I guess I was being unfair. I was trying to go for some humor as it was a very frustrating day we had. But he did tell everyone that he could get this huge fire going in ten seconds - the girl behind the desk, the owner. I think he even told their poodle.

I figured I should restart the conversation. "Jim, I'm sorry - "

He sighed like an actor about to give a great monologue. "I should have never taken you to this lousy bed and breakfast," he said. "I want to drink and you won't let me. I need a drink, that much I can tell you. You've been condescending to me ever since we left our driveway. Every time I try to lighten the mood, you drag it back down into this pit of...I'm not exactly sure what. And you can maybe get out of the chair and help me with this." He gestured to the fire with soot-covered hands. It looked like he had been polishing shoes.

I laughed.

"What?" He said. He tried to sound angry, but it didn't sound right, an uneven keen that didn't mesh well with the rest of the sounds in the room. There were other things around that were heavier than his sadness. The snow outside that I wanted to drown in, the mountains that were taller than I could ever be. I yearned to be smaller than things and I was in a place where I could crouch and duck below most of it.

"Go wash your hands."

Jim sighed and continued to put paper and kindling in the fireplace, stacking it like a sandwich. He truly had no idea what he was doing. But I didn't want to help him. Truth is, I couldn't help him because I didn't know how to start a fire. I grew up my whole life not really knowing how to help with things. I certainly wasn't prepared to help with what was going on right now. I just wanted to sit and watch his limbs awkwardly move. Like rubber or taffy, soft and underdeveloped. It was a really odd thing to witness, let me tell you.

I guess though that I was being a little too harsh. It's my time of the month and I drove here, all three hundred and seventeen miles. I watched him build this sorry excuse of a fire for a bit longer and felt an affection, a tug in the stomach. It's so crazy to me how men really are the weaker sex. I know I shouldn't be saying that, but Lord help me, it's fucking true.

I got up and knelt next to him in front of the fireplace, spaced out the logs a little better. I could smell his sweat, a mixture of salt and oil. He glanced over at me and smirked. It briefly wiped away all the awkwardness, as it always does, but I knew that there would be a deeper feeling, lingering way underneath our skin. I'm not sure if it ever goes away, no matter how comfortable you are with someone. Love can be nothing but sidesteps, like you would in your house, with one person leaving and the other person coming in after work. If you had told me that when I was younger, I wouldn't have listened, but I would have remembered it.

I wiped the soot and dirt away from my fingers, brushed stray bark pieces towards the base of the fire. For a minute there, I thought it would be better if I spread it under our eyes and we could have been warriors, go out in the clearing and fashion spearheads for a raid. I thought of all that snow again and how I would like to traipse in it, make my skin feel a unique sensation. I glanced over at him to imagine him in warpaint. It was weird that I couldn't see it. I thought I married a warrior, but I guess I wound up with a straw man.

He was smiling, like he had found some bygone secret in my movements.

"What?"

"You're beautiful, you know that?"

I know men like saying it because women like hearing it. Some women think it's true and some don't - their humbleness or anxiety does not allow themselves to be found desirable. I find myself not to be beautiful - I am decidedly average and wish I had bigger boobs. I know also that physicality does not make beauty, so I'm not too hung up on appearance. But I know that I am not beautiful. I have written that in stone in my mind. I don't fault him for saying it (it's what husbands and boyfriends do), but I fault myself because I have never told him that it bothered me. It is his go-top cop out phrase to avoid a fight and I don't blame him for falling back on it. But I decided that now wasn't the time and that I better stop it. After all, we were in the mountains, we had time, we had nowhere else to be except in circles around each other, baring teeth. Spearheads, I thought. A warrior raid, I thought.

"Don't do that."

"Do what?"

I sat down cross-legged on the floor next to him. I stared at the logs and patted my pockets for a lighter to make time, even though I've never owned one. Stalling for time, I guess. He sat down next to me and tried to hold my hand, but I brushed him away.

"Saying I'm beautiful. Don't do it, please."

"But you are." His eyes wrinkled into a cute confusion and I almost abandoned this narrative.

But I shrugged my shoulders in a teenage-whatever kind of way. "I'm not so sure that I am."

He sighed and tried to get closer, but I brushed him away again.

"Look, Ellie, I...don't know what's wrong. I know it's been a difficult day..."

"Oh, nevermind nothing," I said and stood up. I walked to the other end of the room where there was some wine that was left out from dinner and started to look for a glass. I couldn't find one, so I ripped out the cork with my teeth. So much talent in this one body, it's astounding.

"Well, you are," he said, still sitting there, frozen, forgetting to move. Maybe those limbs didn't know footsteps.

"What?"

"You're beautiful, Ellie."

"Stop telling me I'm beautiful. I mean it. I'm gonna throw up if I hear that again."

"Alright, what's wrong? I thought you wanted me to be honest with you. I am. I'm being honest. I'm telling you what you want to hear and what it is true."

"There, right there," I said, "I don't want to hear THAT." I clutched the wine bottle harder. I had every intention of drinking it all.

"Well, then, that's just plain confusing," he said, throwing one more stick into the fire. He stood up and grabbed the firestarter from the mantle. "Don't say that you want to hear me say something and then complain when you hear it." He clicked it a few times, lit the edge of the kindling, and the fire went right up, a perfect glow and burn right there just for us. I expected him to turn to me and smirk - almost like a "how about that?" - but didn't, and that made me sad. We were losing moments that we needed to have for our older years.

"I know," I said.

"I mean, you did tell me to tell you anything. You just said that minutes ago."

"I know."

"Well, then..." He stared at the fire, like it was going to provide him with his next line.

The silence rooted down solid in the room, thick for a minute, as I sipped the wine and watched him clean up his mess.

"I'm going to drink," he said with a nod, like he had just got a model train set going.

"Sure."

"You're not going to stop me?"

I held up my wine bottle like I found a missing TV remote control.

"I don't get you, Ellie."

"Well, you married me."

He sighed noisily. "That's what I mean right there. You drive me nuts and you're beautiful at the same time. I love it."

I stood up too fast, hit my shin on the coffee table in front of me. Wine bandage. "Tell me that again, I dare you."

"Ellie."

"I swear to fucking God, say that again."

"Just sit and relax."

"I need to stand is what I need to do. Get on these feet of mine right here." I stood up and fixed myself like I was going to give a lecture. "You only built that fire because of me. Every fire in your life has been me. You've been burning since the minute you knew I even existed."

He held up his hands again. "I'm done. You're drunk. And I need to be drunk, clearly. I've been trying with you, Ellie. I can see that I'm failing. I'm putting the day behind me. I saw that there's a beer place right down the road. I'm going to go buy all of it and then watch this fire."

Jim stood there for a minute, right in front of the flames. I expected him to continue his speech, but he sighed and quietly walked out of the room. It was a shame. I had asked for him to talk and tell me anything, but the minute he did, I realized I never wanted to actually hear it. I knew that from the start, maybe. He had been holding back his entire life until he met me, and when he finally was given a chance to be given a spark and light, I just happened to be the right size of rain storm. Opposites from the start. A gut punch.

I sat down on the couch and watched the fire jump around, gently crack and pop. Jim came back into the room a minute later with his hat and coat on, pointing his keys at me like he had a new toy. It looked like he was finally going to put an ending to his speech, but wound up saying nothing. I almost blurted out an apology but instead I said, "Tomorrow will be better."

He nodded. He blew me a kiss and walked out the door. I imagine he would be out for a while. I sure as hell didn't see any beer store just down the road. He'll find one, though. I heard the car engine start and then fade as the tires crunched over dirt and stone road.

After a few minutes, I got up and carried the wine with me over to the window. There they were, the same mountains I spent all my life wishing that I could climb, or at least get close enough so I could feel them, let the roughness of the rocks scratch my skin. Perhaps if I was rough and damaged and worn, then maybe I wouldn't appear so beautiful anymore - not just to Jim, but to everyone. I could be some kind of woodland creature, waking up to and with them every day and being able to bask in what they might offer. I always had adventures in me, brewing ever so carefully. Maybe this was the moment to give birth, to open myself up and be daring and different. I liked the sound of it, so I went outside, clutching the bottle.

It had begun to flurry, some snow fairy giving her all just for me. I walked for a little while in the backyard of our bed and breakfast, feeling nothing but cold, letting it burn me. I always loved how it could do that, like if you've ever held ice with salt. I looked up and felt so insignificant, a crumb on the planet. Jim was, too. The owners were, too. Maybe they were beautiful and maybe they weren't. But we were all spilled out together on this canvas, like Lego pieces needing to find a spot on the board. I laughed. I finished the rest of the wine and I positioned the bottle to stand in the snow as a marker. Battleground, I thought.

I turned and looked towards the mountains once more. There's rocks there, and peaks, and all sorts of jagged somethings, but there were also answers, sunlight, unobstructed views where humans felt clarity, felt some kind of sense. I smiled. Maybe coming here was the right thing to do. Maybe baring oneself in an alien environment is what you need to do to shed yourself of your insecurity, your stupid dumb blood and skin. Paint, I said out loud. I need paint.

I knelt down and pushed enough snow out of the way to get some dirt or mud. The ground wasn't frozen yet so I managed to get a big clump. I put it on like makeup under my eyes - delicately and boldly. I let my hair down. I took off my sweater and draped it over the wine bottle. I picked up a rock I found. Spearhead, I said, and I slowly walked to the front of the bed and breakfast where the cars were parked. I was going to wait for Jim, I decided. I didn't want a little straw man for a husband, nor did I want a drunk one. I wanted a warrior who would drink blood and hold my hand as we went through this life together, unafraid, ready to move obstacles.

I crouched behind a bush on the edge of the parking lot. I held my spearhead. I felt the mud becoming a new skin. This is how I think we'll be spending the rest of vacation.

I waited in the snow. He was going to come back soon. Any minute now. Soon, he would see that I was more than just a wife. More than just a woman.

FISH GHOST

My sister spoke of a fish ghost that occupies a nearby river. She raised her voice as if her sentences had a weight. But in reality, she's timid.

"It has bones and fins," she said, "but it is poor at cutting through the water."

"Amanda," I said as she swayed, a wind tearing through my hoodie that she always wore.

"Something like an urban monster." Her eyes widened.

"Legend, you mean."

"Whatever."

It's possible she's correct. There's always been rumblings from neighbors and lifers that there's a creature existing in our milieu. Cameras mysteriously break when one gets close to it and they say that we get more snow because of it. All sorts of things like that. I'm a skeptical one, but I take facts over hushed whispers nine times out of ten.

"So is it a fish or a ghost?"

"It's both," she said.

"How can it be?"

"I don't know. Because it can be."

Amanda loves a good fantasy, though, so I let her tell me this as we let the night pass on our grandfather's porch, counting little stars and corn stalks with cold fingers. Even though she's dressed warm, she's still stricken with chills, and I go to give her my flannel as well. For once I'm not drinking, but she's having her share and mine too. The dead soldiers clink like perfect wind chimes. There's nothing else to do but drink and talk of a better life. It's more fun than you think.

"Maybe it's time to go to bed," I told her. Because I knew where this was going. She was going to tell me the history. She was going to tell me how it was born and how it became so ugly. How it was a metaphor for us, or something we were supposed to be - how WE have bones and fins too and are poor at cutting through the water. It was going to take up hours I didn't have.

"No," she said quietly. "No," she said again after a while.

She was beginning to enter a haze. She's been through some trauma and when she gets fixated, I know it's better to leave her alone for a while. I knew she was warm and she had one beer left, so I wished her goodnight. It was important she had some time to sort this out.

After I shut the door, I heard her say, "A mystery. A mystery."

She never came to bed that night. A police officer found her hours later, in the river, only wearing my flannel, with a net she stole from the neighbor's yard. She had been saying different names out loud, but it wasn't of anyone we knew. No charges were pressed, so I went and picked her up just as the sun was rising.

"You don't even fish, Amanda," I said.

"You're missing the point."

"You said it was a ghost. Not even a real fish."

"You're missing the POINT," she said as she punched my passenger side mirror. It hung by a thin cable and clunked against the door every time I sped up. So I crawled as the sticky morning air refused to let up.

"Then what is the point?"

She swallowed a few times. She fiddled with the broken radio and drank from a coffee that I accidentally left behind from the day before. She gurgled it and spat it out the window. I just kept driving because I wasn't sure what else to do with my hands or body, and I knew she was preparing to let loose with some kind of storm. I kept straight on the highway until she unbuckled and told me to pull over.

I did so and parked at this abandoned farm that's been empty ever since we were born. Ghosts, too, or just smarter people than us. Amanda punched the dirt and rocks until her hands bled. I couldn't stop her, she didn't want to be stopped. People who have been hurt and want to hurt don't want to be told no. They want to continue until they are out of words and out of energy. Our point as those who are not hurt need to just shut the fuck up. It's important to know us. Even if it's about a fish ghost or not. Even if it's about something that's not even there. And if it was, who was I to tell her no? She was better than me. Stronger than me. Not my place to tell her anything different.

She held up a clump of dirt and let it sift through a trembling hand. "You know it's there, right? You have to know."

"Yes," I said.

"We're going to go back tonight."

"No problem."

"Bring your shotgun," she said.

"Sure, I said."

She picked up a rock and began to throw it at me, but stopped herself.

"The shotgun," she said again, louder.

"I'll bring it."

She nodded and smiled. "We have work to do," she said.

I picked her up off the ground and told her everything was alright. I put her back in the car. She needed to get some rest.

"You're the best brother in the world," she said as we began to drive off.

I nodded. Even with her eyes closed, I knew she saw it. Or maybe she was imagining something in the water below me, as she stared at it, hungry, wanting to defeat it, wanting to defeat whatever story she didn't want to hear anymore. I've been there. I had bad ones, too.

But hers is one that needs to be stopped. Hers is the one that remains. Even if it's not important to anyone else. It's hers that needs to be heard.

I gripped the wheel. I felt something was chasing me.

THICKER SKIN

When she was biting my neck, I thought of the time that I wasn't allowed on the merry-go-round because I was too tall. She tried to draw blood but I pushed her away. I wasn't into blood during sex yet. I looked at her but she started to move down to my chest.

I remember the white horse with the chipped-paint eyeballs, the burning feeling of standing there and having the carny tell me, are you kidding me, dude? I was barely thirteen, but I guess that's more than enough reason for some people.

She asked me if I was alright.

I said yes.

She said, do you want to try candle wax?

I said I would try anything once, except blood.

She nodded and got up, went to the dresser, lit a candle, and waited. Her bony, off-centered back, her short haircut, the veins visible, the skin glistening, all from me, from a desire for something new.

I remember staring at the carny and balling up a bony fist but knowing full damn well I wouldn't strike him. I remember him sneering. He said, keep going, there's other people in line.

I heard her say something but I did not ask her what she said. I rubbed my neck, numb from her love. I guess it wasn't too bad. Maybe a little sore. Enough to make me know I wasn't in some weird dream. She came back with the candle, ready to drip. I closed my eyes and did not want to see it fall.

When the wax hit my neck, I thought back to the horse, its old, ordinary mouth teeming with splinters and bugs, begging for a rider. I went up to it and the carny grabbed my arm.

Don't wince, she said, it's alright.

I remember seeing the carny grow tough, mangy. I shook him off and got on the horse.

She let the wax harden on my neck and I felt her kiss my cheek, her perfume encircle me again.

The carny said, get the hell off there. I kicked him in the shoulder. I remember thinking that this would get me in trouble.

She picked the wax off, rolled it into an orange ball and set it on the bedside table. She said, do you want to try it again?

I said, let me try it on you. She was eager.

The carny regained his composure and grabbed me around the waist like he was going to slam me to the dirt. The music started up, the creaky organ wailing its creed in the sharp sunlit air, its sprawl spilling out to all others there. Hey, I said out loud. I'm young again. The carny tightened his grip and we began to revolve.

She was on her back now, clutching the sheets, anticipating the pain. I took the candle and I let it drip onto her chest. Her muscles tightened. I didn't realize I was licking my lips. She pleaded for me to do it again. I said I didn't want to burn her. She said, who cares.

The carny screamed to the operator to stop and out of the corner of my eye, a blurred form appeared, a man, security. I told them one more minute, I'm young again, damn it. The carny lifted me off the horse and he nearly dropped me and I almost hit my head on the horse next to me. The acne on my face hurt. I felt security climb on and he smelt of cotton candy.

I let it drip on her ribs, the tiny flame so close to my hand it was singing my knuckles. I set the candle down in a glass holder and I kissed her as she murmured the pain she needed to murmur for years, never close to this pain ever, needing to have it in order to have more. I was glad I could help, but I began to think I wasn't doing this right. I wondered why our first time couldn't be normal, by the numbers. But I needed to stop thinking because it wasn't proper. We were both into growing thicker skin, so there was no better way by making a scar or two.

They both got me off the merry-go-round and I may have elbowed one of them by accident because I smelled blood and saw it on my t-shirt afterwards. They picked me up and threw me as far as they could, the carny sneering, the security wannabe growling because I tested his mettle, or lack thereof. They told me to leave. I pointed back at the horse and told them that they needed to paint it.

We kept kissing. I made my chance count. We finished rather quickly, but it didn't matter really. She told me she loved me, which I'm pretty sure was her moving too fast, so I nodded and told her that I wasn't too big into the candle wax after all.

I called Mom. She picked me up and she had grocery bags all over the back seat. She said she was going to make dinner and she asked me why I had blood on me. I tried to tell her the story but I choked halfway through. We got home and I went upstairs to change my shirt because she said we had company. When I came back down, I saw my older brother and a new girlfriend sitting at the table. Mom started to make dinner. The girl introduced herself to me, her hand smooth. My brother got up to help Mom. I sat down to talk to her. The girl started to light the candles on the table, and she smiled as she did so. Picking up old pieces of wax, she asked me if I had a good day.

THE BOAT OVER THERE

My husband wanted to rest. I said, no, not yet. Not until we get to the boat over there.

I knew it had been there for some time. I knew it was our way out. So resting was not an option.

But I knew once we got out and down the river, we could talk about all the shit we needed to talk about. How we were going to eat, how we were going to catch rainwater. How we would stop the flowing pus and open sores. How to keep predators at distance.

"Swing low, sweet chariot," he cooed.

"Shut up," I said.

We had only been together a year. We hadn't figured out most things yet. It's a shame, he's so sweet, but he needs more of an edge. I am more refined. I am a knife. He's a stick.

I turned around. He was a lot younger than me. But he's just as slow. Because we acquired the same wounds, bled our blood. With a good downwind stream, maybe we would hit our old camp in two days. Surely they would recognize us. We had warpaint and bore barbarian-like jewelry on our wrists now, but we still carried the same affable charm that got us into the group to begin with.

I just wish we never went into that abandoned store. I just wish he dodged instead of parried. I also just wish that I didn't lose my train of thought.

Pushing through thorns and nearly falling to one knee, the boat was indeed still there. It definitely wasn't going to take you on a cruise, but it was going to take you somewhere. There was just enough gas in it to get us to where we needed to go. I had hoped to find more, but I also was looking for cigarettes and a vibrator and found neither, so that's how it goes.

"Andrea," he panted. I could tell he was in pain.

I turned around again. He was getting whiter in the face, weaker in the movements. If he made it ten miles, I'd be shocked.

"Get your ass in that boat and start that motor," I said. "There's no time to play."

He laughed and winced. Blood painted his teeth. "They should have made you a general in Vietnam," he said. "Maybe we would have won."

I smirked. "Come on. Let's get home and fix you up."

Supply missions never get appreciated. If you bring home a box of crackers and some rags, you get a golf clap. If you bring home nothing, you're vilified. But if you bring home two death wounds and a shrug, you get a brief funeral around a Duraflame and become a hero. A disgusting legacy. I'd rather have the crackers.

We clamored in, just big enough for us both.

"Start it."

He pulled at the rope like he was a horny schoolboy.

"Jesus, Cory," I said. It took a few tries, but it went.

The boat sputtered, lurched, almost kind of vomited in a way, but found its footing and went slow down the river.

When we were away from any adversaries, I took a moment to look over Cory. He was fucked. He was pouring sweat and the bite marks on his neck and rib cage were breathing almost, thick with pus and blood and already, vibrant and teaming. Infection these days do not take long, and when it gets to the heart, there's no stopping it. I sighed. He was a temporary husband, but I wanted him to last longer than a calendar month. I tried to cry, but I couldn't bring myself to it. You lose so many people, so many things, that after a while, it becomes a nuisance. You don't even want heaven or a warm bed after the shit you go through. You just want to get home.

He felt my pity. A weakness on my own part. He was going to die on me, though.

"I love you," I said without thinking or meaning it.

He jerked forward, as if the thought made him animatronic.

"Sure," he said.

"I do," I said, softening.

He waved me off and made this bizarre lip-smacking motion. Fighting for air. "I fucked up. How many times can you give your love to a fuck up?"

Should have dodged instead of parried, I thought. But I couldn't say it. I put my hand in the river alongside of me and let the cool water wash off the sweat and salt on my skin. I let it glide over my calloused fingers. I smeared my warpaint with my finger and then used it to trace my apologies on his lips.

"I'm sorry," I said.

He waved me off again. "Tell everyone I said hello," he said. "I haven't got long."

"No," I said, my voice cracking.

"At least let me die with dignity. Don't lecture me like you did the rest."

"I wouldn't dream of such a thing," I whispered.

He eventually passed out. Blood congealed around him and in the boat. It thickened and created a lacquer of sorts which was good so the boat didn't get any holes as it went its course. After a while, I shed my clothes and let my hair down and straddled him. He moaned a few times, but I assured, whispered in his ear that this was how warriors died, and I continued to give him anything I could as our boat continued the path. How I continued the path. How I managed to create the right amount of distance.

The water, thankfully quiet, allowed us such a moment.

BAD DAY

We hired the cleaning girl on Monday. By Thursday we wanted to fire her. She hadn't stolen anything. But we just didn't want her around anymore.

I have to explain some things first. We are very successful people. We are considered to be pioneers in our field and have sterling reputations. Certain people call us for our opinions on delicate matters. We went out and worked for it.

I know people these days don't want to hear that kind of language - "work ethic" - but it's the truth. I will take facts along with my six figures. My wife does the same - she actually gets paid more. So, in conclusion, we can afford cleaning girls. We have obtained that luxury. It means we are able to show our strength off. We can get away with it because any Google search tells you, quite emphatically, that we are respected figures. We keep people employed.

The point, I feel, is made.

It doesn't mean that's it all perfect, though.

Our being rich didn't mean we didn't have our disputes. I spoke to my wife about the cleaning girl by the poolside as the sun beat down on our bones and hurt our tanned skin. It was just about the end of summer. We had to take advantage of these autumn lazy days as best as possible before the busy season. We don't have kids or canvas bags for grocery shopping. We weren't those types of people. We just had a problem. The problem was that we weren't used to change. But we just had a real big change happen - our old cleaning girl died a few weeks ago. The newspaper told me the reason but it didn't just add up to me.

"How should we tell her?" I asked my wife as I sipped the Tanqueray. She sat in the chair reading a magazine.

"Tell whom what?"

"The new girl. Whatever her name is." I took off my Maui Jims and wiped the sweat away. I tried to tune out the radio but it was hard. It felt like flies buzzing in my head. It's why I'm drinking so early. It's why I always drink so early. Sometimes, a drink and some sunlight helps one be rational.

"What do we want to tell her, dear?"

I pointed towards the house with my cocktail glass. "Something is just off. I don't know. She's nice and all but I don't think this should go on. I can't put my finger on it. I think she has to go."

"You find her attractive?"

"I didn't say that."

"You're intimidated."

"Go back to your magazine, Beth," I said. "I'll figure out a way to take care of it."

"Well, then, just do me one favor when you decide to do whatever it is you're going to do," she said.

"Which is?"

"Be sure to use words." This is why my wife makes more than me.

So Friday morning I waited until Beth went to work and I found the cleaning girl taking the trash out of our upstairs bathroom. She was dressed really cute today - a black tank top and these hot pink shorts. I couldn't remember her name to save my life. I stood in the doorway and scratched my arm, watched for a minute, and then spoke up.

"I don't know if this should go on," I said after all.

She was white. I don't know why I should mention that, but I feel that I should. She was possibly in college but probably not. I never thought to ask. This just seemed like the kind of job to me that people take if they're trying to get through school. I wasn't sure if she would be the type of girl that was constantly on the phone, not knowing how to do anything other than to make duck lips in shitty pictures. She braided her hair that day for some reason. I liked how she did it but I could never tell her that. Instead, I just shuffled my feet.

"Is something wrong?" She said. "Was it something I did?"

"No, I just…well, I just made a mistake," I said. It's not often I make mistakes. I'm extremely well regarded in my world. It's worth mentioning again. I'm on a lot of websites. That's how you know you make it big. You let your morals go if it means more clicks.

She put the trash bag down. If she looked in it, she would have seen my Rogaine and my wife's wrinkle cream. I'm pretty sure she's seen the other things we've tried to hide. Whether or not she told anyone else, it didn't matter. But for some reason, this girl's opinion of me really mattered. I felt anxious out of nowhere and I knew that this was going to turn into a bad day. I scratched my arm again, this time a little too hard. "Come on outside for a minute. By the pool."

"The pool?" She said.

"Yeah, come on down. Water's nice. Come on, it's ok. Take a load off."

"I'm confused," she said, "I…"

"Just for a minute. It's a break. Take a break for a minute," I said and she followed me downstairs and through the back door, out to the patio. The pool guys were here early, cleaning and doing whatever, and I turned on that big radio we had to my music, instead of my wife's bullshit. I motioned for the cleaning girl to sit in Beth's chair and I walked over to the portable bar.

"Drink?" I held up the tongs for the ice cubes. I gave them a few test clicks to show that they still work. I was hoping she would laugh at it, but she didn't.

"Isn't it...a little early for that?" She fiddled with her braid. She had it laid over her right shoulder. I'll tell you flat out, that's the kind of stuff that makes a man excited. Especially on a warm summer day. The hot pink shorts helped, too. I felt like I was eighteen again. I got a frenzied feeling stewing hard in me and so I grabbed the Tanqueray.

"I don't know," I said. "I'm going to have one. I always have one around this time."

She shrugged. Maybe she wasn't a drinker. Give it time; she would be.

As I made my gin and tonic, I watched her gaze into the pool. It seemed like at one point in her past she had been all water, the way she stared at it. Like it had all the answers to help with her young life. I was being too judgmental, perhaps, and Beth has accused me of it; but I can't help it. I have to judge in this world - I've made a killing off of it.

"Go on, go for a swim," I said.

She snapped out of her trance but stayed quiet. Studying my face, she watched me drop two ice cubes in the glass and sit down in my lounge chair. The radio crackled a bit. The pool guys went away for a break, I guess, so it was just us two. The sun was hot but I didn't mind it. It was like everything felt new again. All that existed was me and a young girl, a drink and the music. I really did feel eighteen again. I had left my phone in the house and I sipped the gin, let the tangy bite take me over.

I could tell she was nervous, though. She sat up quickly. "I should get back to cleaning up. I have so much to do yet," she said.

"It can wait. We don't make much trash. We're not here often enough." I sipped some more, taking larger gulps than normal. My heart raced. I really wanted her to like me. Beth wasn't here and I was free to be a different self, someone who didn't sit in boardrooms and compare business cards with another. I worked up the energy to say, "So are you in school?"

"Uh, yeah," she said after a pause, and, comfortable enough with the subject, gave a few really strong nods. "Columbia. Art."

"No shit, an art student. I never had the flair for it. I always was better with money. I'm in business."

"I know. You're very big," she said indifferently.

I chided myself for being boring. I finished the glass of gin but didn't get up right away for another. The music drifted in and out, past us in a summer-sweet sway, and I looked up into the sun. A few seconds without glasses won't hurt you. If anything, it makes you see things better, and maybe it would help me figure out this girl better.

"Listen, uh...I'm sorry, I'm totally forgetting your name."

"Ada."

"Ada," I said, nodding. "Now that is a name you don't hear very often. I like that name. Ada. Ada the art student. Now that...that's nice. I mean it."

I was losing her. My lame attempt at comedy was pathetic. Her eyes darted from the house to the pool to the bar back to the house, never stopping on me. Her attention was elsewhere and it was all my fault. I got up quickly to quell the embarrassment and made myself another drink. I dropped the tongs and as I bent over to pick them up, I heard her get up from the chair, a loud squeak ripping through the clarity.

"I should get back to work. I have a lot to do. I appreciate the break, though." Ada said and she began to walk back inside, fiddling with her braid. I had probably scared her to death. This was uncomfortable for her and it was my fault. I wanted to let her know that it was alright and that I didn't mean anything wrong by it.

"Ada," I said, a little sharp. I put the tongs down on the bar and took a few steps towards her. "Look, I'm sorry. I've been a little under duress lately."

She stopped and looked at me, but said nothing. Obviously, I would have to work a miracle to break away from the awkwardness I created so easily. I needed to reach into my business personality, find the perfect language, cajole with just the right emphasis on the right syllables.

"It's just been really nice to talk to someone who isn't a part of all this," I said, motioning to the house. It's the second nicest house on my block, I will admit. Some baseball player and his ten children own the number one spot. I'll find a way to one-up them, eventually. "Beth works too often and it's just weird enjoying the summer alone."

"I can see that," Ada said timidly, nodding. Now she started scratching her arm.

"Look, forget about the inside. Forget about the trash. Forget about all of it." I knew right then and there that I wasn't going to fire her. I did have intentions of it, I can tell you that much. I do it all the time. Anyone slips up in the office, it's instant. I don't make excuses for them. But now, I just felt different. I wanted her to enjoy herself. This wasn't a pleasant job. I wanted to change that.

"I don't understand what it is you want, exactly. This is uncomfortable."

"I know. I'm sorry. Come have a drink," I said, turning back to the bar. The pool guys were starting to come back through the gate, laughing and eating some kind of junk food. I didn't want them here anymore. I was just starting to break through with Ada and I didn't want anyone else to count this as part of their moments. "Hey, guys," I said.

They both looked at me. They squinted in the hard sun.

"Take the day off," I said.

I'll say it diplomatically, they weren't from around here in any sense of the word. So they chuckled and looked at each other to figure out what to do.

"Get on now, take the day and go enjoy it. I'll pay you, trust me."

There still was nothing. I looked back at Ada, who fiddled with her braid again. There was just something about that braid that I really enjoyed. I wish I could have taken a picture of it but my phone was in the house, no doubt buzzing with emails and texts, maybe fifteen Snapchats from Beth or so. She loves that crap.

"Have a drink, Ada. There's plenty there." I turned to the pool guys. They stood stock still, frozen from indifference. "Look, now," I said, reaching into my shorts. I always carry enough money to pay off someone. A secret I learned from masters years ago. I held up two wrinkled hundred dollar bills.

"Go on now. Buy lunch. Do something. I mean it. You can go home."

On the sight of cash, they walked toward me, thanking me a million times, but I just pushed it into their palms and waved them off. They turned and went out the gate, going off to somewhere that I didn't care where, just as long as it wasn't by this pool with Ada and me. Locking the gate, I went back up the walk and saw Ada pouring herself some vodka.

"There you go, that's the spirit, now. If you're going to college, you'll want to drink. Drink a hell of a lot. That's great advice. I'm well-regarded in my field, you know."

Ada screwed the cap back on the bottle but said nothing. She took a sniff of it, grimaced, and then sipped. Let me tell you - I felt new again. There was no other word for it. A swarm of feelings hit me hard and I felt daring. I didn't even need any gin. I didn't need music. I wanted to go nuts. I didn't think it was going to be a bad day anymore.

"What do you think of that vodka? What do you think of it?"

She paused, still trying to decide what to do. I know my behavior was scary, but maybe she had seen scarier in the dorm rooms. "It's ok."

"Mix it with some tea. Or orange juice. You'll want to mix it with some orange juice. Let me go get you something." I ran back into the house and went into the kitchen to get the orange juice. My phone was there on the center island, buzzing away like I had imagined. I opened it up and saw those damn Snapchats from Beth. Alright, I thought. She'll get a kick out of this one. I came back out and held up the orange juice.

"I'm ok," Ada repeated. "Look, this has been nice and all, but I'm going to go. Maybe I should come back another day."

"Another day? No. Don't do that. We have the whole day ahead of ourselves here. Nice weather. A perfect day for swimming. Look, I'll show you."

I ripped off my shirt and walked past her to where our small diving board was. I never went on the goddamn diving board - I had it installed after Beth wanted to show off her non-existent swimming moves. I kept my shorts on and stepped onto the diving board. Ada still stood by the bar, sipping the vodka, sun glistening where her skin was bare. I thought of my college days. What a goddamn mess that was.

I held up my phone like it was a spear or something. I couldn't open up Snapchat, though. I didn't know how to work stuff like that. I knew how to answer and hang up. That's all I needed in the trade, anyway.

"Ada," I said, standing on the board still, "do you know how to work Snapchat?"

"Sure," she said, still taking liberal sips of the vodka. It must have been getting to her head, because she smiled.

"Can you take a video of this and send it out to people?" She came towards the board and I gave her the phone. I didn't even care if she swam anymore. I just wanted her to be my friend.

After a few seconds, she said, "Ok. Go ahead. I have it all ready."

I gave her a thumbs up and said, "Watch this!" I ran toward the edge of the board and leapt. I slipped and went in head first. What I meant to be a cannonball turned into a half-assed belly flop. But I made a big splash and the cold water was a godsend. It was exactly what I needed.

Underwater, I looked up and saw Ada through the blue. I decided to float my way up to the top. I figured it'd be funny to make Beth think I didn't make it. Maybe Ada would think it'd be funny, too.

Finally, I came up for air and saw Ada still taking the video.

"Alright, how did it look?"

"Maybe you shouldn't quit your day job," Ada said, giggling.

I gave that a good laugh. "Ada, you're alright. I don't want to fire you anymore."

"What?"

"Nothing, never mind. Go ahead, send that off to my wife."

"What?" Ada said again. She finished the glass.

"Beth. My wife. Send that to her. I have her in there."

"Maybe I shouldn't do that. Maybe she'll get mad."

"Send it off," I said, "she'll love it. Here." I waded to the edge, up to Ada's feet. I reached into my pocket and pulled out the whole soggy wad of bills. Petty cash, spare change. I got more, believe me. "Ada, here. I'll give you all this if you send it. I want you to send that video."

She looked at my wild hair, the strange look in my eyes. "I can't take all that money."

"I'll pay you. Here," I said, struggled to lift myself out of the pool, but I finally did on the fourth try. I stood there and counted the soaking wet mound of money. "Four hundred bucks. It's yours. That covers one textbook, right?" And I started to laugh.

She did, too. She laughed like hell. When she calmed down, she whispered, "That is true," and took the money. She walked back to the bar and laid the money out to dry. After a few clicks on the phone, she turned and said, "Ok. Beth got it."

"Amazing," I said and clapped my hands together. "Have another drink."

Ada shook her head softly and shrugged her shoulders. "Ok. Why not."

"There you go. Look, I'm going to do it again. A cannonball this time. Send it off to Beth again, will you?"

"Won't she be mad? I mean, won't she wonder what I'm doing out here?"

I considered it. The gin and the sun lifted me to a great height.

"It's ok," I said. "She'll be fine. It's a good day." I paused. "It's going to be a good day. Right, Ada?"

She laughed.

WE CAN REGAIN ABILITY IN TERRIFIC WAYS

Do you want anything from Barnes and Noble? I texted her. I think I'm gonna go on my lunch break.

We haven't dated in months, she texted back. Lose my number.

I figured I'd still get her a good book anyway. There's a ton at the store.

I found some bestsellers on the front table. They had orange and blue on the cover, so I guess that made them popular. I took them to the counter.

Do you know anything about these? I asked the employee.

Sir, the mask must go over your nose, she said.

Well, she wasn't wrong. The elastic is losing its formidability. I guess we all are.

On the way back to work, I noticed a terrific car wreck. Who knew plastic could wind up in such shapes? I pulled up behind it, noticed a young girl crying in the grass, trauma flowing in and around her. I have had trauma. We all do, it's so modern and vibrant.

Are you ok? I asked.

My fucking car is wrecked, she said.

Let's not be so sure, I said. I walked up to her. I debated waiting until the cops or something showed up, but lunch breaks don't last forever.

Would you like a book? I have two, I said.

A book?

Yes, I have two, I said, showing the appropriate amount of fingers.

No, she said, and went back to crying.

I'm sorry. I just wanted to take your mind off of all this.

But she said nothing. I left and drove back to work. My boss, like creeping death, tutted, pointed to the clock.

Late again, he said.

I was helping a victim.

A likely story.

But I was kind of like a hero, I said.

My boss walked away. But the thought gnawed, sewn its way into my psyche. I helped! It certainly wasn't on my list of things to do this morning.

I was a hero, I texted later. I helped process some trauma.

Seriously, she texted back. We're done, sorry.

I bought you a book. It might help us understand what happened to us. Maybe we can reconnect. Maybe we can learn to move again. We moved so well.

I don't want a book. I don't want other things. I wanted you. And you couldn't give me just you. You always had to give me something else instead of you. And I'm fucking sick of it.

But I gave myself earlier today. I'm learning. We can regain ability in terrific ways.

She didn't respond. On the way home from work, I noticed much more trash than normal on the streets. It was concerning. It made me think of where I grew up. I stopped and pulled over to take a closer look. There was nothing I would have ever wanted, but there was always something in there that someone could use, and I have to admit, it made me feel better. Across the street, there was a bar, and the bouncer was smoking and watching me. And in this, I felt better - I had entered someone's life again, briefly. I waved. He shrugged. I stood in the trash, fiddling with my mask.

THE RACES

This time, Mom got drunk first. In a pink cat-embroidered sweater, she delicately opened the Beefeater, like it was one of those antique music boxes. Dad watched from the doorway, grinning, flipping his mug in his hands, still pockmarked with paint from our chores yesterday. This was breakfast.

Hours later, she's driving. We were off to the races today. She's singing but it sounds like she gargled with gravel instead of Listerine. Her red nails clacked on the dashboard. Dad's fumbling to light their cigarettes. It was a sunny day and the light cut hard into them.

To be honest, and I know you're going to think me an apologist, but I didn't mind them this way. I mean, was it healthy? Of course not. I will say this though – they made sure I was fed, read to, and had good shoes to wear. The drinking never hindered their jobs. They just liked to have a good time. Maybe a little too much, but it was days like this that they really let themselves go. If we were going to the races – they loved going to see the horses – then they were going to have gin instead of coffee, beer instead of apple juice.

I remember on this particular day that I wasn't really enthusiastic about going though. The night before, they got me a Super Nintendo – I was the last kid in my class to have one and I was looking forward to finally playing some of the games they talked about. But, they said, I was still too young to be at home. I almost made the suggestion that I could stay at home and watch the alcohol for them, babysit the beer, made sure it didn't run off somewhere. But I swallowed hard and said sure. They assured me we wouldn't be gone too long. Just to the races. Just long enough to throw some money down.

Mom was usually the better drunk driver of the two, but today, something was amiss. She had swayed slightly on the turnpike and got honked at by a tractor trailer. Dad laughed the first time, but when she did it again a few miles later, he chastised her.

"Debbie," he said, "quit driving like an idiot."

She pouted slightly, held her cigarette like a dignitary. "No one's driving like anything. I just want to get there."

"The track will be there," he said. "Let's make sure WE get there."

She huffed and looked in the rearview. "Sweetie, you good?"

I nodded. I was daydreaming about saving Zelda. I was doing the math on how many drinks they would be having at the track — the more they lost, the more they put down. I looked up and saw Mom still staring through the rearview.

"Fuck," she said.

Dad turned. His open mouth spelled it out — red and blue lights. Not the first time, not the last time.

"Well, you've gone and done it now," Dad said. "I should have driven, goddamn."

"Stan," Mom whispered.

"Pull over," Dad said. "I'll talk. You're slurring like a goofball."

The sun highlighted their faces and I remember thinking about how old they looked, how in the kitchen just an hour ago, they looked youthful, like they had just met at a school dance. But now there's wrinkles, curves, spots where things like gin and bitters hide, and it made them look so alien – like they were a monster that couldn't scare anyone or anything. They looked like old dogs that would hang out at gas stations and bake in the heat. It was sad. I remember that so well, and what happened next is something I could draw on any canvas with any instrument.

"Well, Stan," she said, as the cop car whooped behind us.

"Oh, Jesus, don't you even…"

"Wanna bet? We can make our own race."

"Awh, hell, Debbie..." Dad smacked his face. The white paint was still on his knuckles, caught in his hairs. He couldn't even wash his hands properly. But they always knew to make more ice. It's weird – we notice the talents in people and they never notice it themselves.

"We're only two miles away," Mom said.

Dad sighed. He smoked his cigarette. He looked back at me.

"Hey. You know how you like going down hills in your Radio Flyer?"

I nodded.

Dad smacked his lips. "This is the Radio Flyer. And we're going down together. You ready?"

"Sure, Dad," I said. "Whatever you say."

Mom took that as her cue. She sped down the road. The cop raced, too. Here we were – the two finest steeds of our time. Galloping. For glory and honor, for that sacred finish line, for the purse, one for the money. Two for the show. Not everyone can win. Mom clacked her nails on the dashboard some more and Dad sat, clutching his seatbelt, smoking away, like he had intentions on finishing the pack right then and there.

I know what you're thinking – about me and them. I'm not going to say they were the best parents ever – far from. But they were mine. I had to hold onto that. There, in that spot, as a kid – I had no choice but to stay tethered. I wasn't sure where else to go. I wouldn't be sure for a while. Just had to accept it.

We picked up speed. It was such a gorgeous day. I pretended I was in my Radio Flyer, like Dad said. We glided past trees. I felt like I was going to win. I couldn't think about anything else. I imagined my name in the newspaper – and the thought warmed me.

IT'S ALL ABOUT THE BREATHING

All the manuals told me how to breathe. All of the books, the websites, the people in my life that went through this shit. The mother hens on my block all said the same thing - leaning on their chipping paint fences, holding hydrangeas and sunscreen and diet powdered lemonade:

"Hannah, this is how you breathe." They looked like a fish out of water.

I'll be thinking how to breathe all right, when I'm done bashing in your face piecemeal, in every scarce dream I get. *I don't want to be shown how. I just want this goddamn thing over with already.*

Jonathan wanted the kid more than I did. He saw it as a way to live a great life. I saw it as a mistake. We were happy. Why ruin it? I meant it ten years ago when I was sixteen, but now? I want a flat, smooth stomach. I got bills to pay. I don't need this.

Dyspnea. Difficulty breathing. As simply as that can be defined.

Jonathan claims he has it because he's smoked his whole life. But he doesn't have someone living inside of him. He said once he heard voices, when he was younger, but he probably just left the television on or something. I hear this thing talking all the time, crying already, as he's swimming and getting caught up in the thought of existing.

He's taking whatever breath I have left just to make baby sounds. Gurgling and growling and swimming. I hear him moving and it's driving me nuts. *What you're saying is not important. You're just babbling. You're not forming thoughts. You know no one's name, not even your own. Stop with the baby sounds.*

It's what I need to say - that's more important. That's why I need air. I need it for when I'm screaming in the hospital later, trying to breathe.

Jonathan works a lot of overtime so I take myself out for walks a lot. He tells me not to but I can't sit still. Too much weight. So I go through the woods nearby, armed with a knife and bug spray. I'll find a rotten log to sit on and I'll breathe like they all said, but I still get winded before I can finish a song on my playlist.

It's here where I count leaves, it's here where I find the number of reasons to convince the world that I'm not meant to be a mother. I'm up to over a hundred. I'm writing them down on paper. Don't tell me I'm not serious.

I'll upload it as a PDF if I have to.

I have a lot of mother friends. They turned out to be amazing mothers. They dropped all their dreams at the door to have their kids. They don't sleep. Appetites change. They don't drink as much, they're more on the ball when it comes to paying bills, they're changing the bedsheets constantly, they have no problem with doing anything their husbands say. The baby and the husband call the shots. When I get together with them, they have lost all sense of risk. They don't do shit on a dare anymore. They just...breathe. I don't know how they do it.

With no danger or fun behind it. They speak their words, but they don't do a thing. They think about glorious things, but lift not a finger to any of them - the only finger-lifting they do is to fetch their man a beer or grab a toy for the baby.

That's no way to live. That isn't for me.

Don't get me wrong - I'm going to have this baby. I don't believe in the other options, I won't even say the word for it.

It will be loved. It'll be fed and hugged and clothed and taught how to read all of those dumb books with the horrible illustrations. It's going to be taught language, how to ignore it, how to twist it for his own benefit. It's going to learn how to deceive, how to lie, how to be stately enough to impress his peers. He will grow up to be just like Jonathan and I.

That doesn't mean, though, that he's going to be perfect. I won't let people treat him as such. When people come over to pick him up and pinch his cheeks and coo in his face - that's when I'm going to step in. He's not a miracle. He's not special. He's a baby. There are dozens like him everywhere. If you want one, you can have one. If you start in March, you can have him in time for Christmas. Expensive, but at least you don't have to worry about gift-wrapping it.

I won't let people tell him he's perfect because he took a lot of my air. He caused me a lot of problems. He made me sit on logs for hours, checking my pulse, a phone call away from the hospital, because I couldn't say one damn thought out loud.

He took away years I planned to be nothing years and it's going to stick in my craw for a bit.

I think I'm allowed that right.

I'm just the only one with guts to say it out loud right now.

I'm not trying to come off as a bitter, nasty bitch. I know I can be, but that isn't the point of this. I'm just trying to talk while I have the voice and energy at my disposal.

Jonathan doesn't listen - he comes home from work, grabs two Lagunitas, and flips on the Playstation. He asks if I need anything and before I can even whisper a pithy comeback, he's on the couch, immobilized, hacking from his supposed smoker's cough. So I'm saying all of this to you because it's driving me crazy. Maybe it'll get back to him and he'll care, maybe he'll even start painting the spare bedroom he said he was gonna do ten fucking times now.

It's just that I've seen too many people have their world come down so far because of something they didn't want. Or something that they thought they wanted and it turned out to be the exact opposite. I've seen enough of it from my mother friends. A few of them have admitted to me that they love their child, but if they could do it over again, they would have just taken the pill, said no, never went on that second date.

One of them even grabbed my hand and pleaded with me to reconsider. Like I said, I don't believe in the other option, so I just shook my head, ran a hand through my hair and gave a sad look. It's funny how people get when they've done something they can never take back. It's like they're finally a real person. I can't explain it. You just have to see it and if you have, then you know what I mean.

Because truthfully, we have no idea what we're doing when it comes to this. We swear that we'll avoid the mistakes that our parents made, or that we'll never force our kids to do anything they don't want to do, but you know we will. We want carbon copies of our beautifully fucked up selves. I've never seen anything like it, how amazingly frail and egomaniacal we are. We just want to destroy, even in the process of shaping and creating.

I must have said that last line out loud, because I heard Jonathan sit up from the couch and he asked me if I said anything. Like he cares. After some silence, he leans back into the couch and opens the second beer.

I'm going outside on our apartment balcony to try to breathe. The stuffy air from these walls is getting to be too much. You're supposed to be able to relax at home - that's what everyone says. *Follow the manuals. Follow the websites and the mother hens that suffer from the empty nest. They'll want to hold your baby. Remember, it's all about the breathing.*

After ten seconds, I realize I can't relax. My head is swimming.

Sorry, I say to the baby sounds inside of me as I reach behind our potted plant for the pack of smokes I bought a month ago and light one up.

It won't hurt. *If it helps me*, I say to my son, *it's going to help you someday.*

THE OLD BRIDE

It was a wedding with no flowers. That was the funniest part.

I can't say that I enjoyed the food. The open bar was alright - no top shelf liquor, the kind of rotgut you find in the kitchen of frat houses. The groom seemed preoccupied with the baseball scores (can't say I blame him, the Phillies were in first place for the first time in years). All the kids there were picking their noses and screeching, all wearing clearance bin pants and ties and dresses. Loud and obnoxious, just supporting my lifelong desire to use birth control every chance I get. You've thought it too at weddings you've been to, no doubt.

Standard fare, a gathering where you can all catch up and trade unfunny stories, but drink for free while you do so.

But you know who did, the only one who actually wanted this? The old bride.

I don't remember who came up with the "old bride" nickname. We all clearly know her name: she's a longtime friend of ours. But someone said it one night when we were coming down from a majestic high and it stuck. We laughed and told the grass, the grill, the patio furniture. Old bride, har har. Something borrowed and blue and fucking old. The other wives didn't think it was that witty, but we laughed our high fucking asses off. It doesn't take much.

I went alone - my wife had the most conveniently-timed business trip in the history of all mankind. But I got dressed in my best, wore the Movado, shined the wingtips, even got my ears lowered. I drank lots of water beforehand and told myself I would drive myself home later.

You can probably guess how well that one worked out.

Despite the high, we didn't abandon the joke. We came up for a whole sidestory about the old bride to entertain us. She was a princess in a castle. She was a war widow. She had been in a coma and fell in love with the first ugly dope she saw upon waking up. She was only marrying for money. She wanted (or desperately needed) health insurance. Had a one night stand with a great guy, had sex, liked the feeling, and settled.

All of these, of course, were not the truth. They were high school sweethearts, made it through college, and actually are really compatible together. But that makes for a boring story (read: the truth), so we have to twist it up a bit. It's not like she knows - it's a carefully guarded secret.

I guess that my immaturity has led to these things - making up things to hurt people for my own amusement. We all do it. Our friends can be boring folk. We can spice it up a little when we're alone and make little jokes. As long as it never gets back to the person, it's all fair game.

She would never know. She wouldn't have time to know - she had a wedding to prepare for.

The toilets at the venue overflowed and all the glasses had water spots.

I can't knock their wedding dance too much. They were fluid and it was clear they practiced. But mine was better. We sang to an original and they picked a shitty cover.

Don't ever pick the cover song to dance to. If you do, you'll lose any past and future respect from me.

They insisted on going to a church to keep it religious for the parents. Which was okay, because it allowed me to zone out through the Mad Lib sermon and reflect on some things.

I'm happily married but I jack off twice a day. It's sad because I shouldn't have to. But there is no sex anymore. I love my wife, who made for an incredible bride. Her in the dress is what I jack off to.

But I see it in my other friends too; both the men and women. Sometimes, they don't have to say it. I can see it in the way they hold their beer or talk on the phone to their children. They're resigned. Weary. Tired of the runaround, everything's mundane. Cubicle slaves, boil-in-a-bag meals, Netflix until ten thirty, generic sex, sleep.

That's us. That's adulthood in a nutshell. I never thought that *Thirtysomething* was actually going to be a reality for me eventually. A lot of people will tell you that it doesn't have to be that way, but I just tell those people to go back to their blog writing. Because those are the types of folks that claim that everything is peachy, that having kids is a miracle, that the perfect weekend is going to craft fairs and having dollar margaritas at Applebee's.

And let me tell you, anything involving Applebee's is not perfect.

I know we're getting older. I know we're doing things we vowed never to do. Save for retirement, put a curb on the drinking (not me).

Marriage is what you get when you want the adventure you seek to just limp to you instead. It's not sour grapes. That's how it is. I hear it from so many people.

I'm reflecting so much that I'm the only one sitting when the pastor asks everyone to stand. I'm sure someone took a picture of it.

And why do we give Jesus and God all the credit at these weddings, anyway? They're not paying for any of it.

I had a moment alone with the old bride towards the end of the wedding. We were at the dessert table and so I gave her the typical compliments on how beautiful she looked. She smirked, but didn't say anything. I guess you get tired of thanking people for the half truth after a while.

A slower song came over the sound system and she asked me very quietly if I wanted to have a dance with her. "He won't mind," she said, "he's checking to see the score anyway."

I took her by the hand and we walked to the center of the floor, bathed in a dimming strobe, flickering in and out as we matched up with other couples, moving in a trance. I had known her long enough for a dance. But I hadn't know her well enough to dance.

I tried to think of things to say to her, but halfway through the song, I gave up. That's when she started to whisper to me.

"I really didn't mind the nickname," she said.

"Oh, I don't know anything about that."

"Of course you do. He told me."

"Well…" I said, the drink finally hitting me as I found myself unable to craft a way out of this.

"It's a game. I get it. We have to play games in order to get through life."

It was one of the wisest things she ever said. I didn't know what else to say so I just nodded.

"Did Erin really have a business trip?" She asked me, referring to my wife.

"I could really use another drink," I said.

She shook her head. "Well, whether she did or not, since we're on the topic of honesty. And games."

"Go for it," I said, grateful the song was almost over.

She smiled. "She was always a filthy fucking cunt."

I was angry, of course, and wanted to say something, but I couldn't. I just kept dancing until the lights came back on. She gave me a peck on the cheek and went to go find her husband. I went outside with a fresh drink and fielded some questions from my friends who saw us dancing. They wanted to know what we were talking about. They wanted to know what it was all about. But I kept quiet. I thought of my wife's dress. Thought about how she was pure. Away from the water spots and lousy music. I drank to her luck.

THERE'S NO ONE HERE BY THAT NAME

"Hello?" I said.

"Darren?"

I didn't know the voice right away. I was too busy watching the kids in the next room over. I just put up the train set and I didn't want them screwing with it. I had my hands tied. But then I knew. I didn't move. I let the voice struggle for a minute more.

"Darren, come on, I know that's you." It was precious. But it was connected to a fire I could not put out. I didn't have the strength left.

The kids were climbing on the coffee table now. I had an open beer out. I always had an open beer out. I didn't want them knocking it on the train set. I wasn't about to go through all that again. They didn't care that I was on the phone.

"Say something, please."

I said a lot in my life but I didn't know what to say now.

The voice got softer. "I love you, Darren. You know I do. How are the kids?"

I watched them throw the dog's stuffed toy around. It landed on the tracks. The dog was oblivious. I wondered if he would maybe want some of the beer.

Soon I would not remember this age. Neither would anyone.

"There's no one here by that name," I said.

The kids laughed.

THE BEST AMERICAN DEATHS OF THE LAST YEAR

My brother always told me to make lists. He says it's very important. So I am going to finally - at least about this. I'm sitting down at the kitchen table. My brother is at work. Dad is in the next room, watching some annoying loud soccer match. Someone's playing someone and I don't care. I have a beer and potato chips and a pen that works and a notebook that I stole from work and the cat is lying down by my feet and I have nowhere to go. It's time to title the list. Night falls and people are screaming to each other in seedy bars and I write about truths that will sting.

The Best American Deaths Of The Last Year

A List By: Me

1. Eric Anson

2. James Butker

3. Joe Rollins

4. Mark Megaghy

5. Peter Dent

6. ---

I guess we'll end there. I can't remember any others.

"Jesus, they almost scored!" Dad screams from the easy chair.

"Shut up!" I yelp.

"Goddamn it, cheer for your country," Dad retorts and shifts his girth in the night.

I crunch a potato chip and I put pen to paper.

Eric Anson sold shitty weed that was probably oregano before classes every day. He always wrapped it up tight in sandwich bags and wore Slipknot shirts that were too tight. But he was funny. Always had a good racist joke in his arsenal. However, he did not have common sense, and one day in January, in the snow, he flipped off a card-carrying NRA member in a Rav 4 and met his demise on an island right outside Kohl's when the third bullet ripped through his trachea and danced out the other side, bone sticking out, spouting obscenities. Parole, restitution to Eric's family, sobbing families in court rooms and several newspaper articles later, the whole matter was forgotten about, and Eric's ashes remain unscattered in a coffee can in his parent's kitchen. He was 20.

"Man, that goalie," Dad tells the air conditioner. "He can play."

The cat nips at my toe. I finish the beer and grab another.

"Get me one," Dad says. I do. He points a claw at the TV. "Sit down and watch this. It's tied."

"I don't care."

"You and your brother and your lists!" He spits the last word out all over the rug.

"I have work to do."

I sit down again. I fill my mouth with chips. I don't have anywhere to go. I don't have a girlfriend.

Ol' James Butker, or Butt they lovingly referred to him as, was a big game pitcher who took our high school to many grand playoff games, where we promptly lost under the guise that we were competitive. It wasn't him, though - he would pitch brilliant innings, mix and match the heater with the curve, but our offense got him nothing. He would always go home afterwards and steal his dad's liquor and cry with a Maxim and wake up the next day, pretending that he was still going to get his NCAA scholarship where he could promptly lose again under a different moniker. But losing senior year proved to be too much, and he took a cheap bottle of wine from his dad's cabinet, mixed it with Aspirin, and decided to join other high-school athletes in the big towel-smacking shower room in the sky. He was 18.

Dad comes up behind me and grabs the list. "What in the hell are you writing?"

"Give that back, Dad," I threaten.

"Jesus," he says, and gives it back. "The wind blew and the shit flew and there stood you. There's a GAME on in the next room."

"Father!"

"Fine," he said, and went in search of food. He stopped to look at the floor. "Jesus, Liam, you have crumbs all over the floor."

"I'll get them later."

"Potato chip crumbs," as if I didn't know.

"Padre," I said.

"I know you will. Goddamn crumbs and goddamn cats everywhere." He stopped to say something else, but thought better of it and left the room. I shook my head and continued the list. I didn't have many more to write about.

Joe Rollins didn't hurt at all. He was a dickhead. He sprayed himself with this terrible cologne and actually read the Twilight novels and it was not to impress the female race. He did it because he thought it spoke of true love. Joey was a hell of a carpenter, actually. He went the wood shop route and created many sets for our school plays but had a wonderful affinity for 1920's porn, a fact that all of us learned at one party when someone went into his room and found what seemed to be an old flapper costume that he had forced his girlfriend to wear during their many lustful (disgusting?) evenings. The embarrassment on Tumblr proved to be too much, and Joseph, in a suit and necktie, crashed his 97 Ford Escort into the school's favorite oak tree three weeks before graduation, and allowed the fire to lap at his soul, dying in a horribly tragic yet unsurprisingly forgotten incident that the district promptly pushed aside two weeks later. He was 17.

I finish the beer and grab one more. Why not?

"GOAL!" Dad bellows.

"SILENCIO POR FAVOR," I shout.

The cat runs into the living room.

"GOD BLESS AMERICA," Dad says.

"PADRE, SILENCIO," I say.

"Cram it," he says.

I return to my work.

Mark Megaghy never had any luck. Born with baseball talent but given webbed feet, Mark bounced around from jock to nerd to goth to junkie before he finally settled in the experimental art crowd, where his thumbtack and rubber band portraits of everyday life found to find its foothold in the never-expanding art world of our hometown. Having dabbled in mescaline and peyote and Bud Light, he had an affinity for jumping off bridges and filming himself while doing it ("a selfie for the thrillseekers", he told me in a FB message, and he had only sent me this after I accidentally drunken liked one of his masterpieces of art, something he had titled "I Am Better Than Bob Ross"). Gravity proved to be the fucking bitch, though, and he had slipped while going off the Keim Street bridge, cracking his head on crackling concrete, and dying in the murky green mere minutes later. He was 24. He had donated his entire body of work to the local community college museum, where it sits in its basement, giving conversations to cobwebs.

I am shaken by the meaty paws of my life-giver.

"We are America, and we will succeed in our wonderful quest to Americanize the game of soccer," Dad warbles.

"Oh my God, Dad. Please."

"Your mother," he says, "will have a fit if she saw these potato chip crumbs around your feet like this is fucking Arlington cemetery."

Without any more goading, I grab the dustpan and brush.

"I know I raised you right," he says proudly.

I sweep them up and dump them in the trash, narrating as I went.

"Now Goddamn," Dad says, "was that so hard?"

"Yes."

"What are you writing?"

I sigh. I give up. I let him pick it up again. He stares at the yellow notebook paper. He reads to himself. Suddenly, you can see he's tearing up. He doesn't know what to say. Finally, he lays it down back on the table. He comes up to me slowly. He hugs me before I can stop him.

"Liam, why are you doing this?"

I guess in the beginning of my narrative I didn't make my motives entirely clear.

"Liam," he says, and begins to cry a little.

"Dad, come on, there's a soccer game on."

"Please tell me why you're doing this."

"I don't know. Because."

He has yet to let go. I smell all of the years on him - years of attempting to make a life, years of alcohol, years of proceedings and restraining orders and dreams that went south. He is fat. He does not shave well. He can't tie a tie. But he's my dad. What the fuck else am I supposed to do? Forget about him? Let him go? We watch movies together. We don't watch soccer. But we go grocery shopping. We do puzzles occasionally. We don't go to the zoo. But we're family. You tell me what I'm supposed to do.

"Liam," he says, and then he lets go.

"Dad, just go watch your game."

He leaves me without another word. He has his pride. He can be beautiful at times. He knows how to lock doors, but he knows how to open them, too.

I stare at the dead soldiers in front of me. No girlfriend to stop me, no nothing to get in the way of anything. One more left in the fridge; Dad won't want it. I stop moving briefly to hear him sniffling in the living room. The game continues. It all continues. We're all just people. Aren't we? I open it up, the cap falls to the floor. The cat thinks he's being fed, so he runs out. When he learns my moves, he just collapses. He is the smartest one of us all, by far. I pet him. I scratch under his chin, his eyes close and I know in this moment he is the happiest one in the house. He's so happy. I cry a little. I stop and I go back to my seat. The list has two more entries, but the last one will be enough for now.

I start writing about Peter Dent.

But why do I do?

Is it because that all of my friends are married or living together? Is it because maybe I do have a drinking problem? Is it because I wait for things that are never going to happen? Is it because I went to a high school where people I know are either dead or in jail? Is it because the people I know - and actually laughed with, actually have memories with - are no longer people, but ideas? Who knows? Who can say? Don't say God. Just don't. Don't do it. It's nothing. It's a life that has parents that are separated. It's a life where a drink becomes the only food. It's what regulates you down to nothing. It's what breaks you down to a thought that the stars don't give a shit about. Remember that. Beautiful girls will walk past you and smile but they will not know what you are all about because you are afraid. It's why you are given a life with opportunity and chance, and all you get in return is silence. It is why you are writing a list about people you know who are dead. It is why you are left behind when the rest of the world flies on their brilliance.

It is why you write about a fucking guy who died who meant everything to you but only means something to you now because you are alone and that no one is around to drill sense into your head that it's stupid.

But it isn't.

I write more about Peter Dent. It doesn't matter what I write.

I count it as a great death.

It is no different than a bellowing laugh into a dark night, into a void where we use silence as a buffer. It is no different than lying when we could just as easily speak. I do not know until the end of my list that I am loudly crying. The soccer game gets muted. The beer is empty. The cat has gone to sleep somewhere else. I am the only thing left in the room, the only piece of shit left alive.

Dad stumbles in. I don't stop him. He reads over my shoulder what I wrote.

"Liam," he says.

I wave him off. I can't see through the tears. He hugs me again. He whispers.

"You have to stop writing about your brother," he says.

ANXIETY PRESS

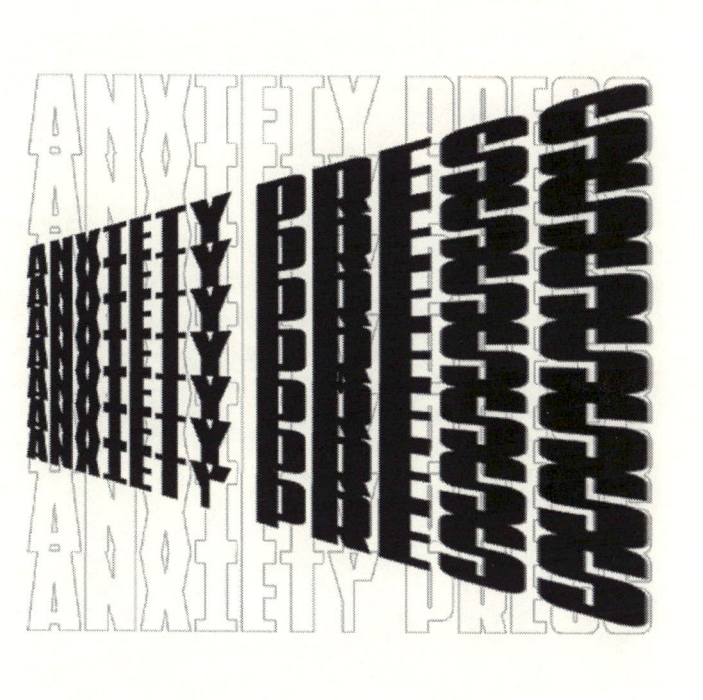

Made in the USA
Middletown, DE
29 March 2024